Janosch
The Treasure-hunting Trip

The Treasure-hunting Trip

Translated by  Anthea Bell

BELTZ
& Gelberg

One day Little Bear went fishing in the river. He was there all day long, but he never caught a single fish. His bucket was empty, he ached all over, there was nothing to cook for supper, and his friend Little Tiger would be hungry. »There isn't any fish today, Tiger,« said Little Bear, »because I didn't catch any.«

And he cooked a cauliflower from the
garden.
With potatoes, salt, and a little butter.
»Do you know what I should like best in
the whole world?« said Little Tiger. »I'd

like us to be rich. Then you could have gone and bought me two trout today. Trout are my very favourite food. Yum, yum...«

»Ooh, yes, trout!« cried Little Bear. He dreamed of catching trout with his fishing rod some day, but he had never managed to get one. Trout are not stupid, and it isn't easy to catch them.

»Fried in the best butter. With almonds and herbs,« cried Little Tiger, jumping for joy and dancing round the room.

»And then we could have cakes with marzipan icing,« said Little Bear.

»Oh, yes, cakes with marzipan icing!« squealed Little Tiger. »I can almost taste them melting in my mouth already...«

»And tomorrow,« said Little Bear, »I'd go straight out and buy myself a rubber dinghy. Because I really do need a rubber dinghy.«

»No,« said Little Tiger, »the first thing we need is a lovely swing seat with cushions, because my rocking chair squeaks so badly. I just can't stand it any more, it's driving me crazy.«

And Little Tiger decided that he would like a racing driver's cap with a buckle on it too, and a red light over his bed, and some fur boots.

»And we'll have smart summer suits made,« said Little Bear, »and we'll wear them to the huntsmen's ball. Oh, Tiger, what fun it would be to step out on the dance floor and do the tango…«

»Come along, then,« said Little Tiger. »We're going to find treasure!«

Next day, Little Tiger went into the wood to pick mushrooms. They sold their mushrooms in the market, and spent the money on a good strong rope, a new spade, and two buckets. You need those things to go digging for treasure.

One spadeful of earth. Another spadeful of earth. One metre down: a hole. Seven metres down: a hole. And still no chest full of gold and money.

While they were digging, they woke up the happy mole, who had been asleep there. He came along and tapped the heap of earth with his stick. »Hullo!« he called. »Is anyone digging down there in the ground?«

The happy mole could not see. His eyes were blind, because he usually lived

underground, where there is never any light. And if there is never any light, you forget how to see.

»Yes,« said Little Tiger. »Bear is digging down there, and I'm up here. We're looking for the best thing in the whole world.«

»Oh, I know the best thing in the whole world!« said the mole. »And it's not down there. The best thing in the whole world is good hearing. I have very good hearing. Can you two hear the wren singing? Isn't it lovely?«

»That's not it,« said Little Tiger. »We're looking for a chest full of gold and money.«

»Oh, that!« said the happy mole. »That's not down there either. I know the ground underground in these parts like the back of my paw, and there's no buried chest here, not this side of the river.«

So they both stopped digging and rowed across the river in their boat.

»Keep farther over to the right,« cried Little Tiger, »or we'll run aground on a sandbank.«

»Do you know what I'm thinking of now, Tiger?« asked Little Bear. »Lovely patent leather shoes. I could buy lovely patent

leather shoes to wear with my summer suit. With white shoelaces. Wouldn't that be nice?«

»Look, Little Bear and Little Tiger!« says the fish in the water. »There's a bottle floating by with a piece of paper inside it. The piece of paper is a map, and the map shows an island with a pirates' cave. There's pirate treasure in the cave, and you can go and get it. Catch that bottle – go on, catch it, quick!«
But it's too late. The bottle has floated past. Goodbye, treasure.
»Too bad,« says the fish. »You silly little things, that's how fortune slips by if you won't listen to what I'm saying.«

It was Little Tiger's turn to start digging on the other side of the river. First Bear, then Tiger.

One spadeful of earth. Another spadeful of earth. As they were digging up the fifth spadeful of earth, along came the lion in blue trousers.

»What are you doing there, boys?« he asked.

»We're finding treasure,« said Little Tiger. »Shall we tell you what the best thing in the whole world is?«

»I know that already,« said the lion in blue trousers. »It's being strong and brave. Would you like to hear me give a good loud roar?«

And he roared so loud that the leaves on the trees in the big wild wood were still trembling like anything three hours later. It was the atmospheric pressure.

»That's not it,« said Little Bear. »We're
looking for treasure. A chest full of gold
and money.«
»Oh, that!« growled the lion in blue trousers. »There's none of that here. I know
everything there is around the big wild
wood, and there's none of that here.«

So they stopped digging and went through the big wild wood.

They walked and walked, for five hours.
They were very frightened.
Are you sure you haven't left your fishing
rod behind, Little Bear?
»Oh, no,« says Little Bear. »I always take
my fishing rod wherever I go.«
That's all right, then.
It was Little Bear's turn to start digging
again on the other side of the big wild
wood. First Bear, then Tiger.

»Dear-me-dear-me-dear-me!« cackled
Dotty the crazy hen. »What are you doing
there, my dears?«
»We're finding treasure,« said Little Bear.
»Gold and money.«
»Gold-and-money-gold-and-money,« cack-
led Dotty the crazy hen. »You won't find

gold down there. The farmer says this
place is no gold mine, and the farmer is
very clever. If he wasn't so clever he
wouldn't keep beautiful hens like me,
would he? Don't you like my hat? I'm
crazy about it! Try somewhere else.« And
she fluttered off.
»Well, let's try somewhere else,« said Little
Tiger.

»Maybe we shan't need to dig so hard somewhere else.«

As they were going along the road, they met Mallorca the travelling donkey.

»And where are you two little things going?«

»We're off to look for the best thing in the whole world,« said Little Tiger.

»You're in luck, then,« said Mallorca the travelling donkey. »I'm looking for that,

too. And I know where it is. It's very far away. You can come with me; I'm going there myself.«

As they went along, Little Bear's paws started to hurt. It was all that walking. »Will you carry us a little way?« he asked Mallorca the travelling donkey. »Donkeys are supposed to carry children, and we're still children, aren't we, Tiger?«

Then they sailed across the sea.

When they reached land, Mallorca the travelling donkey picked up his suitcases and went travelling on, because far away is never where you are.

»I know what!« said Little Bear. »We'll look for treasure in the sea. There's always pirate treasure sunk in the sea.«

Little Little Bear went to catch some fish.
They sold their fish in the fish market,
and spent the money on two divers'
helmets and oxygen packs. For diving.

But there wasn't any treasure down on the sea bed either. No chest, no gold and no money.

And when they came up to the surface again, the big fat man holding a rope with a motor-boat on the end of it laughed at them. »I suppose you two were looking for treasure down there, were you?« he said.

»Yes,« said Little Bear, »because, you see, what Tiger and I need is...«

»Ho, ho, ho! You'll be a long time searching, boys!« laughed the fat man with the motor-boat. »You won't find so much as an empty shell down there. We've cleaned it all out. Hard luck!«

Oh dear. Suddenly, the world was so empty, and the sea was so cold and deep.

And their little house by the riverside
was so far away…

And if the kind big crane had not come flying along and carried them back over the sea, I expect they would have come to a sad end and never been seen again.

»Why are you walking all bent over,
Tiger?« asked Little Bear.
»Because I'm so unhappy,« said Little
Tiger. »Because we haven't found any
treasure.«

»Get on my back,« said Little Bear. »I'll
carry you a little way.«

»Why are you walking all bent over?«
asked Little Tiger.
»Because you're so heavy,« said Little
Bear.
»Stop a minute, then, and I'll carry you a
little way.«
After that Bear carried Tiger again, and
then Tiger carried Bear again, and they
went on taking turns until it was evening.

They spent the night asleep under a big tree, because they were tired after walking so far.

When they woke up next morning, they saw they had been sleeping under the tree where the golden apples grow. What luck!

»There we are,« said the old owl, who was really a tree himself. »That's life. They go running all over the place, looking for gold underground, and where do they find it? Up above them. Things are seldom what you might expect. Things are usually the other way around.«

Straight away, Little Tiger wove two baskets, and Little Bear climbed the big tree. They filled their baskets with golden apples right to the brim. The baskets were very heavy.

»I'm all bent over,« said Little Tiger. »It's

because my basket is so heavy. Do you think you could carry me a little way again?«
But that idea was no good, because Little

Bear was already carrying his own basket, and you can only carry one thing: either your basket full of gold or your best friend.
»I know what!« said Little Bear. »When

we get to town we'll exchange this gold for money. Money is made of paper, it's much lighter to carry, and we'll still be just as rich.«

When they got to town they went to the bank. There was a nice man there who counted the golden apples and said, »Eight hundred. Exactly eight hundred. Eight hundred is twice as much as four hundred, so I'll give you four hundred.«

»Oh, twice as much!« cried Little Tiger. »You see, Bear? We're going to live happy ever after. We've got exactly twice as much now. Isn't that wonderful?«

The money was not heavy. There was only enough of it to fill a bag. They could carry the bag between them, and still have a hand free each, for picking berries.

Near a wood someone came to meet them. »I am on His Majesty's service,« he

said, »and I hear you have money. Half of everybody's money belongs to the King. That's the law. In return, the King will protect you from the robber Rodrigo and take care of you when you are in need.«
So they had to give him half their money, and he hurried all the way round the wood and came to meet them again.
»Ah, we've met before!« he said in a friendly voice. »And as we already know, you have money. And half of everybody's money belongs to the King, that's what the law says. In return the King will protect you from the robber Rodrigo and so on and so forth.«
He did that three times. So how much did they have left? Can you do the sum?
»What a shame,« said Little Tiger. »Your share's all gone, Bear.«
»*My* share?« cried Little Bear. »What do you mean, *my* share? *Your* share's all gone, you horrible, beastly Tiger!«
Then Little Tiger called Little Bear a silly idiot, and they went on calling names, and then they started fighting.

»You foolish little things!« says the bird in the grass. »Each of you fighting his very best friend, just because of money. Tomorrow someone will come on His

Majesty's service again, and you won't have anything left at all. Not even a friend. Really, how stupid can you get?« That night they made friends again, because they were scared, all alone there. And when they were asleep the robber Rodrigo came and stole the rest of their money.

Wait a minute, you rotten robber! Don't

you know that the King protects everyone
who's paid up?
That just makes the robber Rodrigo
laugh.
»The King?« he says. »Him, protect peo-
ple? He's asleep in bed, a long way off, so
how could he protect anyone? Ha, ha,
ha…« And he ran off into the wood, never to be seen again.
So now Little Bear and Little Tiger had
nothing left at all.

»Why are you walking all bent over, Tiger?« asked Little Bear.

»I'm so unhappy, Bear.«

»Then climb up, and I'll carry you a little way.«

After that Tiger carried Little Bear again, and then Little Bear carried Little Tiger again. No more quarrelling and no more fighting. No heavy baskets to weigh them down, and no one on His Majesty's service to take half their money away.

»Oh, Tiger, how nice this is!« said Little Bear, when Little Tiger was carrying him.

That night they slept out in the open. They didn't need to shelter under a tree, and they had nothing left for the robber Rodrigo to steal.

When they got home, they found the happy mole asleep on their sofa. He had taken shelter there from the rain the day before.

»Do stay!« said Little Tiger. »Little Bear cooks such wonderful meals, they bring tears of joy to our eyes. They really do.« So the happy mole stayed.

Little Bear cooked a cauliflower from the garden, with potatoes and salt.

»Tomorrow there might be mushrooms,«

said Little Tiger. »How would you two like mushrooms?«

»Lovely!« cried Little Bear. »And if you can't find any mushrooms I'll catch a fish. And if I don't catch a fish, there's always cauliflower.«

Next day the sun was shining, and it was so fine that Little Tiger didn't go looking for mushrooms. Little Bear didn't feel like fishing, so they had a cauliflower, with potatoes and salt.

»Oh, listen!« said the happy mole. »The wren is singing. Isn't it lovely?«

And they listened to the wren's song, and the sun shone over the meadow.

The bees were humming, and the cauliflower had tasted wonderful.
Mmmmm…how happy they were. How really and truly happy.

Janosch, geboren in Zaborze, Oberschlesien, arbeitete in verschiedenen
Berufen, ab 1953 als freier Künstler.
Er lebt heute auf einer einsamen Insel.
Er veröffentlichte zahlreiche Kinder- und Bilderbücher und Romane,
zum größten Teil im Programm Beltz & Gelberg.
Für *Oh, wie schön ist Panama* erhielt er den
Deutschen Jugendbuchpreis.

Gullivers Bücher (75)
© 1979, 1982, 1990 Beltz Verlag, Weinheim und Basel
Programm Beltz & Gelberg, Weinheim. Alle Rechte vorbehalten
Ausgabe in englischer Sprache
für die Bundesrepublik Deutschland, Österreich und die Schweiz
© der englischen Übersetzung bei Andersen Press Ltd., London
Reihenlayout und Einband von Wolfgang Rudelius. Einbandbild von Janosch
Gesamtherstellung Druckhaus Beltz, 6944 Hemsbach
Printed in Germany
5.90.1
ISBN 3 407 78075 3